The Grass Keeper Chronicles

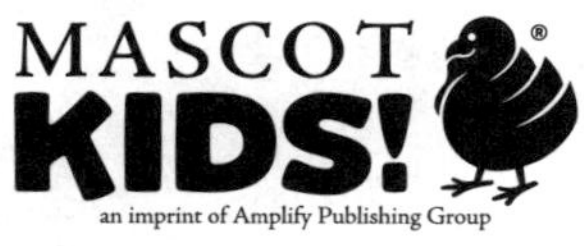

www.mascotbooks.com

The Grass Keeper Chronicles

For more information, please contact:
Mascot Books, an imprint of Amplify Publishing Group
620 Herndon Parkway, Suite 320
Herndon, VA 20170
info@amplifypublishing.com

Library of Congress Control Number: 2021923886

CPSIA Code: PRV1122A
ISBN-13: 978-1-64307-561-7

Printed in the United States

Life is either a daring adventure or nothing at all.

-Helen Keller

The GRASS KEEPER Chronicles

NANCY SHAKESPEARE

THE SHADOWS

The binoculars I pull from my bag are wet, and I use my jacket sleeve to wipe off the lens. Out of habit I'd put on my jacket, but now sweating, I struggle to pull it off. The leaves swirl and dance above my head and for just a moment, I relax. Briefly, I forget why I'm out here, hiding in the woods. A few minutes go by before I press the cold binoculars to my face. I can now see the man's profile more clearly. I shift my weight and start to stand when I hear a door slam. *Mom*. I run back to the big tree, back to my hiding place, back to where I feel safe. I look at my phone. It's 7:30. Dinnertime. Mom is looking for me now. My stomach starts to growl, quietly at first and then rumbling louder. I grab my jacket to buffer the noise. I wonder if he hears me. It will only be minutes before my mom calls out my name and gives away my hiding place. I move in a little closer, but with every step I take, my feet find branches left from last night's storm. They snap under my sneakers. I know being out here is risky, but I need more proof. I pick up the binoculars again, and as I focus, I feel like he's looking straight at me. I duck behind a tree just in time.

"OLIVER!"

Chapter One
HOME

Summers at Nana and Pop's house usually meant swimming in the lake, fishing at Hollier's Grove, and playing in the "bunker" Oliver Morton and his grandfather, *Pop,* had built together. His best friend, Kayden, always came with him. They'd play outside in the warm sunshine all summer. The bunker was their secret hiding spot, a place to pretend they were spies or government agents. Oliver was tasked as the official *grass keeper* of Nana and Pop's garden, as well as maintaining the grass all around the bunker. Over time, it had become overgrown with weeds and tall cattails, and Oliver didn't want to remove any of it. He liked the privacy. It made him feel safe . . . from what, he didn't really know. He imagined the likes of Bilbo Baggins might just pop in one day for a chat or to borrow something. And at the end of August, just when they'd had enough of the heat, they'd fly home in time to catch a Red Sox game before school started. But this summer, there was no Kayden, and this time, Oliver wouldn't be flying back to New England. Lakeside was now his home. Boston was where he was born, where he'd learned to ride a bike, where he'd built his first snowman, where Kayden still lived. Boston was the only life he'd ever known, and Lakeside, Texas, was nothing like Boston. Oliver's Mom called it a "fresh start," but at twelve, he didn't particularly want a "fresh start."

Oliver's dad had taken a *temporary* assignment in Texas so they moved to Lakeside to be near his grandmother. But as days turned to weeks and weeks into months, Oliver knew in his heart that they weren't going back to Boston, and *that* life seemed a world away. Sometimes he'd find himself "zoning out." Most of the time, his *zoning* was at the *wrong* time.

"Mr. Morton, will you be joining us today? And are you and your partner ready to present your project to the class?"

Oliver stared blankly at his teacher Mr. Jackson for a moment before he snapped out of it.

"Yes, sir," Oliver replied. "I'm here."

"This is becoming a habit, Mr. Morton. I *see* that you're *here*. I asked if you were ready to present to the class."

"Yes sir. We're ready," Robert answered quickly for the two of them.

Robert was Oliver's lab partner and was becoming a good friend. Oliver and Robert stood to present their invention. Their classmates continued chattering away. Mr. Jackson gave them all his *this is your last chance* side-eye glance, which meant Mr. Jackson had reached his breaking point. The room went silent as Oliver fumbled to find his composure. But before either of them had said a word, the end of school bell rang.

One by one, Mr. Jackson's class gathered their things. Oliver relaxed and put away his books as Mr. Jackson spoke to the class.

"Well, it seems Mr. Morton and Mr. Polan were literally 'saved by the bell.'"

Laughter broke out as Mr. Jackson attempted to regain control of his classroom.

"Okay, okay, listen up everyone. Tomorrow concludes our presentations. I've loved everything I've seen so far and although I appreciate the effort that's gone into every single one of your projects, I want to stress that you can't do *too much* research, nor can you have *too much* proof! And on that note . . . see you all tomorrow."

As each of Mr. Jackson's students filed out of the classroom, Oliver heard Mr. Jackson call his name.

"Oliver, could I have a moment of your time please?"

He walked over to Mr. Jackson's desk as his classmates scattered. Oliver knew this routine well. He'd say he was sorry for *daydreaming* and that his *daydreaming* didn't at all mean that he wasn't interested in Mr. Jackson's class. And then Oliver would mention how much he missed Boston, and that sometimes something would trigger a memory from back home. And then he'd promise to try harder to pay attention. This wasn't the first time Oliver had been asked to stay after class and he'd had to listen to more lectures than he could count since moving to Lakeside.

"Mr. Morton, I don't know if you're aware . . ."

Here it comes, thought Oliver.

"Well, it's just that I don't know if I've told you what an asset you've been to our class," said Mr. Jackson.

Oliver was noticeably surprised.

"An asset, Mr. Jackson?"

"Absolutely. And even though you've seen me frustrated at you more than once, it's maybe because I expect more out of you. I truly believe you add so much value to our classroom. In fact, I'm quite comfortable in saying that I think you're one of my brightest students," added Mr. Jackson.

"One of your brightest students, sir? I had no idea you felt that way. I was assuming it was about my *daydreaming,*" said Oliver.

"While I'm not exactly thrilled to occasionally have to wake you up from your mental musings down memory lane, I do really appreciate you. And that brings me to the main reason I wanted to talk to you. I'm starting an engineering team to compete with other state schools, and I want *you* to join me. You could also help me by recruiting a few more 'engineering minds' like yourself. They don't even have to be in my class. Honestly, I don't even really care if they're engineering students. Out-of-the-box thinkers come from *all* backgrounds," encouraged Mr. Jackson.

Oliver marveled at the idea. He had only recently started making friends. When summer started, he hadn't seen the point. He knew that by middle school, lifelong friendships had already formed. When he first arrived in Lakeside, Oliver felt like a small fish in a fishbowl full of piranhas. Even though his mom kept telling him that he'd find *his people,* he'd always wondered who *his people* were. Recently, he thought he was finally starting to understand what she meant—making friends with a few guys from school and from his neighborhood. And as Oliver listened to Mr. Jackson, he thought this might be perfect. This "group" could not only help Mr. Jackson, but maybe . . . just maybe . . . they'd be willing to help Oliver too. His feelings about Lakeside were changing for the better and besides, having a few allies *might not* be such a bad idea.

"Sure, Mr. Jackson. Sounds cool. I bet Robert would be up for it too. And I can already think of a few others that might be interested as well."

"Excellent. I was hoping you'd say yes," Mr. Jackson replied.

"Thanks for believing in me, and I promise I won't let you down," Oliver replied happily.

"I'm sure you won't, Mr. Morton. Have a great evening, and I'll see you tomorrow. Oh, and Oliver, be ready to present first tomorrow. If you could, please get your *daydreaming* out of your system before you come to my class. I can't wait to see your design!"

As Oliver left the classroom, he smiled. And he realized it had been a long time since he had actually smiled. He really liked Mr. Jackson. Madden Jackson, or *Madds* as the other teachers called him, reminded Oliver of his grandfather. He only wished Mr. Jackson could have met Pop. For whatever reason, Oliver immediately felt safe with Mr. Jackson, and it didn't hurt that "Madds" Jackson also happened to be best friends with Oliver's other favorite teacher, Mrs. Fedewa. If he did finally divulge his secret to a teacher, he knew he could trust both of them.

On his walk home, Oliver started to think about how he'd pull a team together—a team for Mr. Jackson and a team that could help him with his problem. No one knew his secret. No one. The last few weeks had become more dangerous. At the beginning, it was more like a game that he could set down whenever he liked, but now, here he was, trying to solve a mystery, a mystery that no longer could be solved alone. He had to tell someone. Someone who could keep a secret. Someone who could help. Someone like . . . Kayden. Oliver decided there was no one better to share his secret with than Kayden. He always had the answers. Over the years, they'd had lots of adventures together. He thought about the snowball fights they'd have on a cold January morning. And then after racing to the town center to Mike's Bakery, they'd find just enough money in their pockets to have one cannoli each.

And then obviously shivering, Big Mike would make them sit outside. They didn't care. They were drenched, but the warm cannolis and the cups of free hot cocoa were all they lived for. And as he dialed Kayden's number, a number he'd dialed more times than he could count, he really wished he was here. Kayden was always the "brave" one of the two of them. They'd watch scary movies (never at Oliver's suggestion) but Kayden couldn't ever stay awake, leaving Oliver wide awake and alone, his nails bitten to the quick. Kayden and Oliver had been best friends since kindergarten. And when Kayden answered, Oliver wasted no time.

"KK, I have something unbelievable to tell you, but you can't tell anyone. It's a matter of life or death," said Oliver.

"Life or death?" Oliver could hear Kayden laughing, probably at what he usually described as Oliver's *overactive imagination*.

"Seriously life or death. I've seen something I shouldn't have seen. At first, I was excited and I thought it might be fun to investigate, but now, I'm not so sure. I'm feeling . . . I'm just feeling . . . Honestly, I don't know what I'm feeling, but I know that I'm no longer safe. And to top it off, I think I'm being watched. I'm scared," Oliver continued.

"Dude, you're *scaring* me. *Now*, you're going to *have* to tell me everything," said Kayden "and don't leave *anything* out."

Oliver spoke a mile a minute as he told him what had happened over the summer and of his conversation with Mr.

Jackson. And when he finally took a breath, he realized he only heard breathing on the other end of the phone.

"Kayden? Are you still there?" Oliver asked worriedly.

And after what felt like a lifetime, Kayden replied.

"Wow. I mean . . . why haven't you told your mom or dad or even the police? Didn't you say your friend, Robert's dad was a police officer? Like why not tell him?" asked Kayden.

"Yeah, he's the chief of police, actually. I don't know. I guess I'm just nervous. I don't know who will believe me, but I guess it doesn't matter anymore. I have to share my secret because I can't continue to do this by myself. I'm getting paranoid about everything," Oliver replied.

"This is crazy, bro, but I agree. This isn't safe to do alone anymore. This is the perfect opportunity to pull together a tribe. You know everyone would be up for it and you'd probably score points with your teacher," said Kayden.

Oliver liked that . . . "tribe." That was fitting. Even though Kayden had never *officially* met Oliver's new Texas friends, clearly he too thought they could be trusted.

"Here's what I think you should do. First of all, since Mr. Jackson will probably want to know who you've contacted, you need to decide who you want in your tribe. And since next week is Thanksgiving, I'll be in town, so I can help too. Isn't your cousin Patrick coming? If so, I'd definitely tell him. Next, call everyone and tell them to meet us at the bunker on Sunday. That way, we can work out a strategy and catch this scumbag! Gotta go, my mom's calling me. Later, Loser. Kayden out."

As he hung up with Kayden, Oliver already felt a little lighter knowing *his secret* was not such a *secret* anymore. Kayden was right about everything. Oliver knew he was the right one to call. And he was right about Patrick. They'd always been close. They'd even grown up on the same street. However, Oliver was a little bit worried Patrick would accidentally *spill the beans* to the rest of their family. But in the end, he decided the relief was worth the risk. As he got ready for bed and turned on his lamp, Oliver really started to believe everything would be okay.

He pulled out his notebook and started to create his tribe. Now that Kayden knew, he'd tell his friends Carter and Pierce on Friday on the way to school. And Harry was Robert's older brother. He was only a year older but much more *mature*, plus Harry knew everyone in Lakeside. *Mr. Popular* is what Robert always called him. Harry and Robert lived down the street from him, and Oliver was fairly confident that they could keep a secret, even from their police chief dad. If anyone would be able to solve this, it would be . . .

The Tribe!

Chapter Two
FAMILY

It was Tuesday, and Oliver shot out of bed. Usually, this time of day brought him little pleasure . . . going to school was not anything he'd looked forward to lately. But today, he felt good. He felt far less worried, ready to write the next chapter.

"Rise and shine, Scout. Time for school," bellowed his mom from downstairs. "Dad is on the computer 'Zooming' with your sisters. He wants a word before school."

Oliver bounded down the stairs. He couldn't wait to tell his dad the news, although he hadn't yet decided how much *news* he was prepared to share.

"Girls, your time is up. Let Oliver have a chance to talk to Dad now. Please finish getting ready or you'll be late for school . . . again."

"Ooh, Mom, do we get to take the car today?" Hattie asked excitedly. Suki's ears perked up.

Gretchen Morton was usually the calm one in their house, but Oliver could see his mom was clearly becoming impatient with her daughters this morning, repeating the same thing for what Oliver believed to be "like the tenth time this week." He quietly murmured alongside his mom's explanation to his sisters.

"Not today, girls. Remember, we agreed to Fridays. How many times this week have I said this to you both? We are waiting on your grades to come in," said Oliver's mom.

Begrudgingly, they headed upstairs to finish getting ready, trying to knock over their brother as he rushed to the computer to tell his dad his good news.

"Hey Dad!" Oliver excitedly beamed to his dad. "How's Brazil?"

"Hey, Scout. Thank goodness for technology. The quality's so clear. It's almost like we're just sitting in the kitchen, talking. Scout, you'd love it here. The people are friendly, the weather is fantastic, and the food in Brazil is . . . 'muito bon,' which is about all, sadly, I've managed to learn in Portuguese. It means 'very good.' Hey, I was just telling your sisters that it looks like I may get home earlier than expected. Maybe even as soon as Thursday. I'm so ready to get home. How's school?" his dad continued.

Corrin Morton travelled a lot more since their move to Texas. Oliver and his sisters hated that he was always gone, but they loved the travel "pressies" he always brought back with him.

"Good. School's good. Actually, school's better than good. I almost forgot to tell you. My engineering teacher, Mr. Jackson, just asked me to put together a team to compete," Oliver announced.

"That's awesome, bud," said his dad proudly. "You've said you like this Mr. Jackson before."

"Yeah, I do. I think you'd like him too and Pop would've really liked him. Apparently, according to Mr. Jackson, I'm an *asset*. That's what he called me. An *asset*," Oliver continued.

"Nice. I like Mr. Jackson already. Correct me if I'm wrong but it sounds like you might actually be considering becoming an engineer like your old dad after all, eh?"

"You never know," said Oliver.

"Well, whatever you do now or later, I couldn't be more proud of you! I know you've had a tough start and you think you don't have anything in common with anyone in Lakeside, but can I assure you that you do. Texans are loyal people," said his dad. "In fact, the love of my life is from Lakeside!"

"Yeah, I know. Mom pulled out her yearbooks to show Hattie and Suki last week. Did you know Mom was a cheerleader? I didn't even recognize her!" said Oliver.

"Oh yes, they say everything is bigger in Texas, and that definitely applies to your mom's hair in middle school! Scout, I know you need to head off to school soon, but I just wanted to quickly remind you that I need you to help me. Please look after our girls until I get back and keep up the good work at school! You're really impressing the teachers—and me, for that matter! Also, I know I say it a lot, but Mom really needs you a little more these days than usual, especially with all my travelling. She misses Pop a lot, and this move has been hard on her too," Oliver's dad urged.

"Don't worry. You can count on me, Dad," Oliver replied.

"I know I can Scout. I can always count on you, and you can always count on me too," his dad added.

"I'll Zoom you tomorrow after I know more about the engineering group. Miss you, Dad."

"Sounds good. Good luck. Miss you too, bud," his dad said, waving as he logged off.

After all that had been happening in Lakeside, Oliver really wished he had more time to talk to his dad. Just quick conversations with him always made him feel a bit better. As he stood in the kitchen, staring out of the window, daydreaming, his thoughts were interrupted by a car horn. He grabbed his bag and hurried outside, attempting to beat his sisters to the front.

"Shotgun," Hattie yelled as she swung open the door.

"Sorry guys. Not today. I have a presentation at work and I need the whole front seat to myself this morning," said Oliver's mom.

Clearly annoyed, his sisters hopped in the back seats and Oliver joined them. Oliver was close to his mom and knew she missed her dad. They had been really close, especially since she was an only child. His mom juggled a lot and Oliver knew he and his sisters should help more.

"How is your Dad?" his mom asked as they drove to school.

"He's good. He's learning Portuguese," replied Oliver.

"Portuguese? Well, that's good. It's at least a Romance language. I've been trying to get that man to learn Spanish since we found out we were moving to Texas. Maybe this will motivate him. In fact, you all should be taking Spanish . . . not French," said his mom.

"Although, since you have so many French speakers in your house, you should be 'acing' French."

"Yeah. Yeah, we know, Mom. But we can't take Spanish," replied Hattie.

"Is that because *Miles* isn't in Spanish?" Oliver commented as he rolled his eyes.

Oliver knew way more about Miles than he cared to know. His sisters were completely obsessed with him. He was the captain of the high school varsity soccer team, so basically *everyone* knew Miles. Only Oliver also knew Miles worked out at exactly 7:00 a.m. every morning. And that most of the time, Miles played some sort of rap music when he worked out, and that in addition to soccer, he was also an amazing swimmer. And he also knew that Miles went to bed at 9:00 p.m. and that Miles left his bathroom light on all night. Oliver blamed his knowledge of Miles's morning and evening routines on his sisters for *accidentally* waking him up . . . and keeping him up . . . with their ridiculous *oohs* and *aahs,*

and he blamed his parents for putting him in the room on the east side of their house . . . a.k.a. the west side of Miles Hunt's house.

"What ever happened to playing hard to get?" asked Mom.

"Too much work," said Suki.

Oliver knew better than anyone that his twin sisters weren't interested in any *extra* work. Suki and Hattie were in high school and were identical. Both had long, dark, straight hair with deep, hazel eyes, just like his mom. Oliver looked more like his dad's side of the family with his blonde, wavy hair and blue eyes. His sisters were very petite like his mom, and Oliver seemed to have gotten his dad's height because he was almost as tall as his twin sisters, and they were four years older. In addition to their looks, Suki and Hattie also did everything else in a very "identical" manner. They both made cheerleader and had also both managed to fail physics, which was one of the only high school classes that Oliver thought actually sounded interesting. And they were part of the Lakeside "scene." It was as if they had been here their whole life. They loathed the "family" carpool, but no longer bothered complaining because they knew that if they hadn't both failed physics, they'd have had their own car by now.

As they pulled up to the high school, both girls gave Oliver a quick tap on his head and hopped out of the car.

"Good boy, Scout," Hattie and Suki chirped in unison.

"Mom, really? I mean they do this every day. I'm not a dog," complained Oliver as his sisters continued to "pet" him and laugh.

They think they're so clever, Oliver thought to himself as the girls skipped off to catch up with the rest of their "mean girls" posse.

"Mom, why are high school girls so weird? All they do is look at themselves in the stupid mirror, putting on stupid make-up and brushing their stupid hair. Did you know that they count their brush strokes, and did you know that they make videos showing the same stupid things they do every single day? I don't get it."

"Yes, I do know that. But Oliver, you *do* know that I was one of those *stupid* girls when I was younger, right? Also, there's no point in trying to figure us out. You'll spend a lifetime trying to understand us. Just ask your dad," Oliver's mom replied.

The girls spent hours and hours primping, and when they were finished, Oliver always thought they looked exactly the same. Their *routine* was actually quite comical though. And his sisters *could* be helpful from time to time. But the best thing about Oliver's sisters was that *most of the time*, they left him alone.

Chapter Three
SNOOP

Oliver had been keeping a very detailed journal of the "case" he was building. He coded and catalogued everything, something his grandfather had taught him. And Oliver found comfort in what he knew best. His mom called his investigating "snooping," but he thought of himself as more of an "adventurer" like Pop. Since his death last year, Oliver found himself thinking about his grandfather often, especially when he was in his bunker. He often wondered if Pop ever felt scared when he was alone gathering evidence.

Paul Oliver Patterson was a good man. He was fair and kind. He was born and raised in a rural town in the North of England. Pop knew from an early age that he wanted to travel the world, and so he was happy when at eighteen, he was forced to enlist in the British Army. After studying science at Imperial College of London, he rose through the ranks from General to Colonel in record time. and became a scientist. He moved to Paris on assignment but soon fell in love with France and with beautiful Sophie Barnard. Oliver's grandmother was a nurse at a local hospital, and after a chance meet and a brief courtship, the two of them got married. Oliver's mom, Gretchen, came soon after and the three of them would have lived happily ever after in France, but Pop was transferred to the US. So, when Oliver's mom was around five, they packed their bags and moved to Texas. They quickly adapted to the warm weather and warm people of Lakeside.

Gretchen was a lot like her dad. When she left for university at eighteen, in addition to getting a degree, she wanted to see the world. And after moving to Boston to go to school, Gretchen fell in love with New England. In graduate school she met her husband, Corrin. And ironically, now here she was back in Lakeside to raise her own children in her childhood home.

Because of his job, Oliver's grandfather had lots of "army gear," and when he died, he left it all to Oliver. He'd often pulled out Pop's old leather wallet. In it was a photo of the two of them fishing and a photo of Pop in uniform from the 1960s. Oliver wanted to be just like him. And out of everything Oliver had from his grandfather, his binoculars were, by far, his favorite. He took them with him everywhere. His grandfather had carved in his initials, though his initials could only faintly be seen these days. Oliver spent hours combing through articles about his grandfather, and because Pop spent so much time in France, there were several documents written in French. Even though his mom was French, Oliver was determined to translate the documents himself. He had even signed up for French at school. And it was French class where he met his friends, Carter and Pierce. Oliver had desperately wanted to tell them his *secret* and now, after talking to Kayden, he was happy that they'd soon know. He decided to tell the two of them on Friday. He worried what they'd think about the hours he'd spent peering from his bedroom window, gathering *evidence*. Would they think he was obsessed or weird? He'd honestly started to wonder himself.

* * *

As he watched the man getting out of his blue pickup truck, Oliver jotted down on his weekly agenda, *"Secrete—Vendredi."* Since it was only Wednesday, he had two more days to figure out how to start that conversation. He could show them all of the dates and times he'd seen the man. He'd even sketched a few drawings of the tattoo on the man's arm, nicknaming him Tattoo. As he looked through his binoculars like he'd done so many times before, he prayed someone else was watching and would come forward to take that burden from him. He wanted to believe someone else must have seen something. But he knew it wasn't likely as he'd been watching him for over a month.

Oliver decided to move a bit closer and found a tree that gave him the perfect point of view.

He could see fairly clearly without his binoculars, and as he peered around the tree, he could see clearly two letters on the blue work shirt the man was wearing. It was *EP*. He wondered if those were initials or a company logo. He watched as the wind grabbed the brown, yellow, and red leaves from the forest floor and swept them up in the air, only to land haphazardly back all over the ground. Despite the fact they were technically in fall, last night's storm had brought back all of the mosquitoes. Oliver had forgotten bug spray and he swatted the swarms of mosquitoes away from his face, trying not to draw any attention. He took a few steps closer. *Crunch*. He had stepped on another branch. Apparently, the branches were part of the storm's destructive path as well and had made a mess of his bunker and the area around the shed. The hot air had made his body sticky and his stomach wouldn't stop growling. He clutched his jacket to his stomach. He knew it must be close to dinnertime, and he could smell the pizza all the way out in the forest. He knew it was only moments before his mom would yell out his name and he started gathering his things.

"OLIVER!"

"OLIVER!"

He was still so amazed that his tiny mom could produce so much sound, but her shouting for dinner was something that always reminded him safety was around the corner.

He looked but didn't see Tattoo. Nervously, he looked through his binoculars to see if the man had heard his mom yelling, but he didn't see him. Oliver wondered if he'd gone. Just then, he heard the sound of an engine and saw the man drive off in the blue pick-up truck.

As the man drove away, Oliver thought about the blue shirt he was wearing. It was some sort of uniform. Maybe he was a mechanic, or maybe he worked at a gardening center? He had definitely seen that uniform. He couldn't think of any company with the EP logo or initials. Maybe Harry or one of the other boys could help with that. Not only did Oliver feel certain he'd seen him before, but he felt even more certain that he'd see him again. He wondered what he'd do when he *did* see him—confront him with all of the "evidence," freeze in fear, scream for help? He knew he needed to think of a plan and not panic when he eventually did see him again.

Quickly, he ran to where the blue truck had been to see if he'd left behind any evidence. And after searching all over the ground, he went over to the small shed he'd seen Tattoo go in and out of many times. It was locked. He had almost decided to call it a night when out of the corner of his eye, he noticed a rock that looked out of place. He nervously lifted up the rock, looking around to make sure the man hadn't come back. He was so nervous he nearly dropped the rock on his foot. He couldn't believe it. Right here, not even one hundred yards from his own house, was a key. It was getting dark fast, so he wasn't completely sure, but he initially thought the key looked pretty similar to their mailbox key. *It must open the shed*, he thought. Darkness had now covered the forest in a veil that was impenetrable to the flashlight Oliver had with him. He would have to come back more prepared next time.

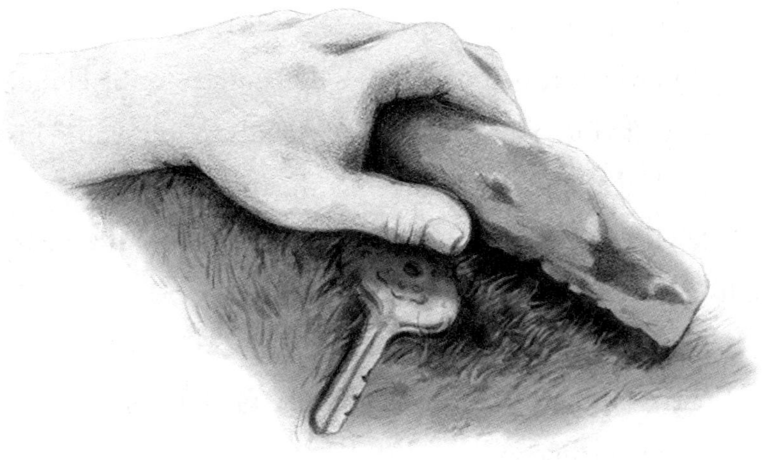

Oliver reached into his jacket pocket to find his own keys and pulled the mailbox key from his keychain. He then *temporarily* put his key in the other key's place under the rock. Now, he'd just have to find a way to make a copy of the key and return the original. But he knew he'd need to act fast because the man would come back soon looking for it.

Oliver's night of evidence collecting was over for now, but

he felt confident this key would open the shed and lead him to more evidence. He just needed to find a way to get it copied. Putting the key on his keychain, he rushed toward his mom and the delicious smells coming from his house. Fresh pizza beckoned him into the safety of the kitchen.

"Dinner's ready," said his mom as he sat down at the table. "Everyone, please wash their hands. So, Scout, what type of snooping have you been doing today?" asked his mom.

"No snooping, just exploring," he replied.

"Well, why is it that you always do your exploring alone? Why don't you invite one of your friends to join you?" his mom asked as his sisters walked in the room.

"Hey loser. What friends? Wait . . . news announcement. Oliver now has friends?" Suki joked.

"When did the amazing occurrence happen?" added Hattie.

The two of them pranced around the kitchen, pretending they were putting on a theatrical performance.

"And what's all over your face?" added Hattie.

Oliver went back to the hallway bathroom to look. His face was filthy, and he brushed off a little, but he left just enough to wind up his sisters. A little dirt never bothered him.

"Girls, be nice. I love the fact that your brother spends so much time outdoors. When we were young . . ."

"We know, we know. When you were young, there were no electronics and people played with sticks. We've heard this already. Your life must've been so boring, Mom," Hattie continued.

"Boring? It was definitely not boring, but there are no Tik-Toks to prove it. I know, why don't the three of you go get us some ice cream after dinner?" suggested his mom.

"Fine," said Suki, agitated that they had to include him, but always happy when they got to take the car.

And after dinner, they headed out the door.

"Bring me a scoop of vanilla, please," yelled his mother as they raced away.

"Can we run by Home Depot while we're out? I need some things for my engineering class," Oliver asked his sisters.

"Sure, Scout. We'll stop on the way back. Mom gave us twenty dollars. If that's enough to cover it, it's cool with me," Hattie replied.

He rolled his eyes and gave his sisters a *thumbs up*. He hated how everyone still called him *Scout*. He must be the only middle schooler with a dumb nickname. But this time, he didn't say a word. Just knowing he'd be able to put the original key back soon without anyone noticing helped bring him a sigh of relief. He shifted the key in his pocket. He wasn't going to let the two of them ruin this. He'd come way too far to let any cross words from his sister get the best of him.

Chapter Four
THE SHED

It was Thursday, and Oliver's dad was finally home. Since his parents had decided to go out for dinner and drinks to celebrate without kids, Oliver decided to take advantage of the time. He'd managed to return the key the night before, but discovered Tattoo had moved the shed. Oliver made a list of places Tattoo could have safely and swiftly moved the shed. Realizing he only had limited time before his parents would be home, Oliver knew he needed to use his time wisely.

So, as he'd done countless times before, Oliver jumped on his bike and headed to Hollier's Grove.

Hollier's Grove was a wealthy area where some famous architects and engineers had recently set up a campsite to work on Lakeside's new downtown Plaza Hotel. Oliver and his friends liked to skateboard in Hollier's Grove, and he'd seen tons of makeshift buildings all over the campsite. He

thought it would be easy for Tattoo to sneak *in* a shed without drawing any attention, and that it would also be easy for Oliver to sneak *into* the shed if it was there. And because it was only two miles from his house, Oliver felt it was as good of a place as any to start.

It was dusk when he finally arrived at the campsite. There was music playing and people milling about. The architects and engineers looked like they were having fun, and it made him think of the stories his parents had told them about going to weekend-long festivals at campsites, dancing, and listening to music.

As he crept onto the campsite, he noticed one particular shed was slightly smaller than the others and that it was a bit off to the side from the rest of them. He thought that could be the one, but it was too dark to tell. He'd need to get closer. Oliver slowly approached, being mindful Tattoo could be watching. He looked around as he put the key in the lock . . . the door opened. He could hear magical Disney music playing in his head in this 'eureka' moment.

Oliver slowly twisted the knob and as he stepped inside, he felt confident he'd find all of the evidence he needed. But the door abruptly shut behind him and a darkness filled the space. He pulled at the door. It was locked. His mind raced. Without any light, he wondered how he'd see what was inside, and even more importantly, he worried how he would get out. He tried to focus with only thin bands of light coming from underneath the shed door. His hand slowly felt the surrounding walls for a light switch. Nothing. *Tic toc, tic toc.* He couldn't see a clock, but he felt like they were all around him. His phone. He had a phone, a luxury Pop never had, he thought. He illuminated the small storage room.

As he scanned the room, he noticed long white tables covered with items. Walking from table to table, he realized he was now looking at the Smith's grandfather clock, Mrs. Gunn's silver, Mr. Zuniga's baseball card collection, the Donald family's Scottish plates, Mrs. Hunt's antique paintings, and even Mr. Jackson's porcelain cat figurines. Everyone's stolen items were here. He quickly took pictures with his phone.

Once he had taken as many photos as he thought necessary, he tried the door again, and it still wouldn't budge. His parents would be home soon, and Oliver knew they'd be worried. The realization that he wasn't getting out of there until someone opened that door made his stomach upset. He heard voices outside the door, and he knew Tattoo would most likely be the person to open the door next. Frantically looking around for somewhere to hide, he found a crawl space underneath one of the far tables and jumped under just as the door opened.

Through the door walked two men. He recognized one by his shoes. It was definitely the man he had nicknamed Tattoo. His mind was racing, and his heart was beating so loudly he wondered if anyone could hear him. Having a hard time concentrating, he tried to focus on his breathing.

"What's with the sudden sense of urgency?" asked Tattoo.

As he froze in fear, Oliver tried to learn more about the other man, but it was too dark. Looking at his *fancy* dress shoes, Oliver decided the other man was most likely in a suit. Their "day jobs" might help determine the direction the tribe went for the case. So now he had Tattoo and Suit. Oliver hadn't actually thought of *him* as having an accomplice because he'd only seen Tattoo, but it did make sense. So many houses were hit. *Actually, Suit could be the one in charge*, he thought to himself.

"Because the cops are closing in. They've been questioning everyone and have even been at the school multiple times. And this campsite will be closing soon. They've broken ground on the hotel. We need to move the unit tonight," Suit reported.

After he spoke, Oliver thought he recognized both Tattoo and Suit's voices, but he couldn't be sure. The panic of being discovered consumed his thoughts. Suit had mentioned "the school" and Oliver wondered what he meant by that. He knew the police had visited all of the schools, but why would either of them know about that? He then wondered if they could be talking about *his* school? And what, if anything, could someone from his school have to do with this?

"Just hold tight. We have one more and then it's over. One more. You can hold out for one more, right?" Tattoo urged.

Suit was silent and the change in the timbre of his voice led Oliver to believe he was a little worried. Suit paced back and forth right in front of the table where Oliver was hiding, and Oliver could hear the desperation in his voice as he replied.

"Just one more, but then, we need to move."

"All right," agreed Tattoo. "Let's get out of here."

And as the door was inches from closing completely, Oliver put his phone in the space at the bottom to hold it open. He couldn't believe all the evidence he'd found. He couldn't wait to tell Pierce and Carter about Tattoo, about Suit . . . about everything.

Chapter Five
THE SECRET

Today was the day he'd tell Pierce and Carter. He just hadn't quite figured out the best way to start up the conversation. *Hey guys, so one night when I was NOT minding my own business, I started spying on someone and saw him do something terrible. And instead of telling anyone, I watched him do it over and over again. Yeah, I didn't tell anyone.* What would they think about their "snooping" friend?

Fall was here, and the trees looked almost magical with the Spanish moss draped from each tree branch. As he looked out his kitchen window, Oliver thought about how he used to love being outside. In Boston, although he'd be bundled up in layers of clothes by now, he'd spend every waking hour outside. He loved the fall. The trees and leaves were changing colors here and there was just enough of a breeze to need a jacket in the early mornings and evenings. Everyone was out walking their dogs, smiling as if it was a newfound activity. He was seeing more and more neighbors these days, neighbors (and dogs) he'd not noticed before. And because of the stifling hot summer, most hadn't ventured outside. *I can tell*, Oliver thought, *because the doggies are slow and extremely plump*. Lakeside really was beautiful, and the warm weather should bring him comfort, but Oliver couldn't shake the nagging feeling that Tattoo was watching him. He had felt *his* "presence" for the last couple weeks. Oliver visibly shivered as he finished his breakfast and headed outside to meet up with Carter and Pierce.

The boys walked to school together most days lately. They met between their houses, at the corner of Ashcroft and Porter, so today wouldn't be any different. Only Oliver knew today *would* be different. He was nervous. He didn't want to be late. As he approached the corner, he felt a chill and looked around.

“Morning,” they all greeted each other in unison as they headed toward school.

Oliver didn’t waste any time.

“I have something to tell you both, but you have to swear you won’t do or say anything unless we all agree, okay?”

“Dude, what are you talking about?” asked Carter.

“Just swear,” Oliver urged.

“Okay, I swear,” said Carter.

“Pierce?” inquired Oliver.

“Yeah?” Pierce answered.

“Swear you won’t do anything with the information I’m about to tell you,” Oliver repeated.

“Scout’s Honor,” Pierce replied and chuckled. “Get it . . . *Scout’s Honor*?”

"Yeah, I get it," said Oliver. "This is serious, Pierce. I'm worried we're being watched."

"Seriously, Ollie, now you're scaring us. You look like you've seen a ghost. What's up?" Pierce replied.

Oliver felt like he *had* seen a ghost, and his body felt clammy. A bead of sweat rolled down the side of his face as he started.

"I have something important to tell you guys, and it's going to blow your minds. The only other person I've told is Kayden," said Oliver.

"Go on," Carter urged.

Oliver paused to look around before continuing.

"You know all of the robberies in Lakeside?"

"Yeah. The Smiths live next door, and someone took Mrs. Smiths's grandfather clock. Why? Did y'all have a break-in too?" Pierce asked.

"No, we're fine. Nothing has happened at our house. It's just . . ."

Oliver paused and looked around before finishing.

"It's just that . . . well I think . . . actually, I *know who* . . ."

"Know *who* what?" Carter asked.

And right as he was about to tell them his secret, out of nowhere, Robert and his big brother, Harry, jumped out from behind the bushes.

"BOO!" shouted Robert.

The three boys jumped up so high in the air that they looked like if a strong enough breeze hit them at that very moment, they might actually fly.

"Gotcha!" Harry echoed.

"Sheesh, guys! Want to give us all a heart attack or what?!" asked Pierce.

"Whoa. Whoa. Easy partner. What's up with you guys?" joked Robert.

"If you must know, Oliver was about to tell us something very important," said Pierce.

"Something important about what exactly?" Robert inquired.

"Actually, it's *who*, not *what*," Carter corrected.

"So, *who* is so important? Come on. Tell us. We won't tell anyone," Harry continued.

"Yeah, you guys really are acting strange," Robert added.

"There's no *who* or *what* to talk about. It's just been a weird day, that's all," Oliver answered.

He didn't think he was ready to tell his secret to everyone yet, even though he knew he could trust them both. He decided after this, he would suggest to Carter and Pierce that they all get together at his bunker. Now just wasn't the time.

"Whatever, dude. All I can say is that this has seriously been the strangest *morning*," said Harry. "Was last night a full moon or something? First, my alarm didn't go off this morning, then I went to pour the milk, and it had strangely frozen in our fridge, but everything else in the refrigerator was fine."

"And then walking over here, we saw a black cat run past us, hiss, and then dart up a tree. I hope it's not a bad omen," Robert added.

"Na-Nu Na-Nu," chanted Harry, making "this is crazy" gestures with his hands in the air.

Bad omen? Oliver seriously hoped that wasn't the case. He definitely didn't need any bad omens right now.

"You guys are giving us bad mojo," said Pierce. "And besides, we're going to be late to school if we don't leave right now."

Oliver was slightly relieved Pierce spoke up. He'd decided to tell both Pierce and Carter later, and then they could all decide when to tell Robert and Harry. He hoped all of these "weird" occurrences were just coincidental. Oliver had always been told that bad "luck" comes in threes and there had already been two! He tried to brush those thoughts away as they walked inside the school, because he knew today was way too important to get sidetracked.

Chapter Six
THE DISCOVERY

When the boys stepped into the foyer of their school, they spotted the police officers. Another robbery. He knew the whole neighborhood felt violated. These visits from *Lakeside's Finest* had become a regular occurrence. Most of the time, the boys didn't even take a second glance, but today, they stared at one another because they understood. Oliver could tell they did. It was different. He knew his friends could see that Oliver was holding a secret that was bigger than he could handle alone. Pierce and Carter had homeroom together and they headed off to their classroom.

"See you at lunch," Carter shouted to Oliver as he winked.

He was ready to tell Carter and Pierce his secret. Lunch. He'd tell them at lunch. He'd tell them everything. He was left alone and as the morning announcements started, Oliver opened his locker to put away his backpack. Until Oliver heard him clearing his throat, he hadn't realized that Principal Sanders was standing right behind him.

Christian Sanders had been one of Oliver's mom's best friends growing up. Apparently, they had even dated for a while. That always weirded Oliver out, but Mr. Sanders was nice enough most of the time. Oliver had even thought about going to talk to him, but since he'd had been in Principal Sanders's office multiple times this year regarding his *day-dreaming,* Oliver thought it best to wait.

"Good morning Mr. Morton. How is your day going? And how is your mother? How are y'all adjusting to country life?" said Principal Sanders.

"She's good," answered Oliver.

"Please give her my best. And how's your dad? I really have loved getting to spend time with both of them. I think your dad fits right in with us here in Lakeside. And your sisters too. Pretty different to Boston, eh?" said Principal Sanders.

"Yes, sir. It's a nice town I guess," Oliver mumbled.

"Well, I wonder if I could I trouble you for a moment in my office?" Principal Sanders added.

Oliver looked for support from his friends, or anyone for that matter, but no one was there. He was all alone and knew he didn't have an option.

"Sure thing, Mr. Sanders. Let me just put my bag away."

"Actually, why don't you bring it with you," urged Mr. Sanders. "We can talk in my office."

"Yes, sir," said Oliver

Oliver wondered if Principal Sanders could hear his heart beating. He felt like he might faint and had to hold onto his locker to steady himself. As morning announcements echoed throughout the halls, Oliver knew that once his secret was out, things would never be the same.

The rest of sixth grade raced to class as the final bell was ringing, and Mr. Sanders continued to talk to Oliver as they walked.

"I just need to talk to you about something that has come to my attention. And don't worry, I've told Mrs. Fedewa that you'll be a little late this morning."

He was sure that Principal Sanders knew. The thought that this no longer would be *his* secret made Oliver relax a little. But as Oliver stepped into the principal's office, everything seemed off. His relief turned to fear, and then to confusion. One of the police officers he'd seen in the hallway earlier was now inside Principal Sanders's office and everyone, including Mr. Sanders's secretary, had very serious expressions on their

faces. What do they know? What was about to happen? This wasn't what he envisioned for his first *secret* "disclosure," and he immediately wanted to run. He wanted to go home. He wanted his mom. But it wasn't until he sat down that Oliver realized it was much worse than he could have even imagined.

Tattoo. It was him. Of course. It was so obvious. The emblem, the EP-initialed shirt, the tattoo that he'd seen so many times before. It hit him like a ton of bricks. Tattoo was Ethan Parsons.

And he'd been standing by the door the whole time. Oliver's body started to sweat, and all he could do to keep from passing out was to focus on the back of Mr. Sanders's computer screen. Mr. Sanders sat down at his desk before continuing.

"Oliver, I think you know *why* you're here, but I would love to hear *your* side of the story."

"I'm sorry, sir. My side of the story?"

He didn't know what to say as he struggled to clear his throat. His hands were now wet with perspiration and nervously, he brushed them on his pant leg. Oliver knew that he should say something, but he couldn't find the words.

"Oliver, I'm sure you've met our custodian, Mr. Parsons, and he was just telling us about the binoculars. We know you have them, but we just want to know why."

Oliver was visibly confused. Did he just ask *"why?"* How

was he supposed to answer the "*why*" question? Was he asking *why* Oliver has been watching from his bedroom, *why* he knows more than he should about the robberies, or *why* he's not told anyone? Wait, did Principal Sanders say binoculars? How did Mr. Sanders know about the binoculars? Had Mr. Parsons been watching him? Oliver was petrified and didn't even know how to start.

"Well, I . . ." Oliver started to speak but was cut off by Tattoo.

"Christian, we've known each other for how long? And you know I wouldn't be here complaining about any little thing. And I also want to say that I'm not even angry that he's taken *my* binoculars. I would just like them to be returned to me because they were my father's," Tattoo said.

Whoa. Whoa. What?! Tattoo . . . or Mr. Parsons . . . was claiming Oliver stole *his* binoculars? Oliver knew what the next question from Principal Sanders would be, and his body tightened.

"Oliver, do you have Mr. Parsons's binoculars?"

"No, I . . ."

How was Oliver going to prove the binoculars were his? Who would they believe?

"So . . . you wouldn't mind us checking your backpack, then?" Principal Sanders inquired.

"Well, I . . ."

And before he knew what was happening, Principal Sanders had Oliver's bag and was searching for the binoculars. Of course, Oliver never went anywhere without his grandfather's binoculars, and Principal Sanders found them straight away. He shot a very disapproving look at Oliver. And then, to Oliver's surprise, Principal Sanders turned the binoculars upside down to see the POP initials. Now, they'd feel silly. They'd see Oliver's grandfather's initials and that would be the end of it. And Oliver started to feel a bit more confident as Mr. Parsons took them from Principal Sanders. He'd see Mr. Parsons was lying. He noticed the police officer just kept scribbling away in a notebook as they spoke.

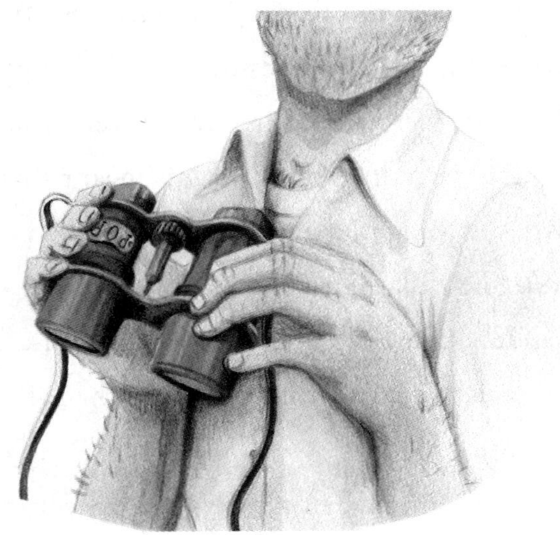

"As I was telling you earlier, there are my father's initials, POP—Peter Owen Parsons . . . carved in . . . right here."

He had thought of everything. Oliver was stunned and now for the first time felt an entirely different feeling. He felt defeated.

"I'm very disappointed in you, Oliver. I know you are new here, but I need you to understand that we do not tolerate stealing from anyone, and Mr. Parsons has been here for many years." Principal Sanders went on to say, "Mr. Parsons has agreed to not press charges so there won't be any record of this incident. However, consider this a very stern warning. Because next time, I won't be as forgiving," Mr. Sanders announced.

Oliver was stuck now, and his stomach started to hurt as he begrudgingly handed Mr. Parsons *his* grandfather's binoculars. He knew what this meant. Not only was Mr. Parsons much smarter than Oliver, but now *he* had the upper hand and *he* knew it. Who would believe Oliver's story? Even more frightening to him was that this meant that he had seen Oliver watching him and would most likely continue now that *he* knew that Oliver knew his secret.

"Mr. Sanders, can I be excused now?" Oliver asked. He thought he might actually throw up right then and there if he didn't leave.

Principal Sanders spoke firmly. "Not before you apologize to Mr. Parsons."

Oliver couldn't look Mr. Parsons in the eyes. He was too scared. He spoke so quietly that one could barely hear.

"I . . . I'm sorry." Oliver was surprised he was even able to speak. And, without skipping a beat, he grabbed his bag and ran out the door.

Oliver wanted to cry, but he knew it wouldn't do him any good. He didn't even know if he should bother telling Pierce and Carter now. He knew they'd most likely believe him, but what could they all do about this injustice? Would anyone ever know the truth? The reality was starting to sink in. Lakeside Middle School had always been a place where he didn't need to worry, where he felt protected.

Now, nowhere was safe.

Chapter Seven
LOVELY

Oliver's mom was in the back garden when he arrived home from school. She was busy planting hydrangeas and he sat down next to her.

"What's up, Scout?"

Scout had been his nickname for as long as he could remember, but he hated that his parents and sisters insisted on calling him that.

I'm in middle school, Mom. I'm not a baby, he thought to himself.

"Nothing much."

He'd felt so sick at lunch that he never even managed to see Carter or Pierce. He'd not been able to tell them what happened in Principal Sander's office, or to tell them anything else, for that matter. Since his mom didn't know anything about the office visit either, maybe she'd still believe him. He wanted to tell her, but "nothing much" was all that came out in response.

"Well, I have some fabulous news. Remember that fountain I was wanting? The one with the little bees and cherubs?" she mused.

His mom loved anything with bees or cherubs, so which one she was describing right now was escaping him. He nodded.

"It's been discontinued, and the price dropped so low, I couldn't help myself. I bought it and it's being delivered tonight!"

"Exciting, Mom."

"And that's not even the best part. I met this *lovely* gentleman today at the shop who offered to install it for me for free."

He was trying not to look like he didn't care. He knew there might be a job in there for him.

"Also very exciting, Mom."

"I had hoped you'd say that because I told him you might

want to help him out."

"Gee Mom, I wish I could help out, but I have so much homework tonight."

Pulling the homework card always worked.

"But it's Friday, silly boy. You have all weekend to finish your homework. I've been looking forward to getting to work with my clever son. With your engineering mind, I figured this would be right up your alley."

Busted. He knew he didn't really have much of a choice at this point, although putting together a fountain was not top of any list he'd ever created.

"Sure thing, Mom," said Oliver.

"Great. They're delivering it any moment so if you want to go grab a snack, everything should be ready to go in around thirty minutes."

"Sounds super-duper exciting, Mom. Can't wait."

"Thank you, sweetie." His mom gave him a kiss on his forehead, the same kiss she'd been giving him since, like, forever.

Oliver headed back inside and grabbed an apple. He climbed the stairs to his bedroom and locked the door behind him. After opening his drawer, he grabbed his box marked "PRIVATE." He opened it up. Inside, he found the key, his notepad, the extra lens for his camera, and where his full pack of gum usually was, he found a crumpled-up pile of wrappers instead. His sisters had been in his things yet again.

"HATTIE! MOM! Hattie was in my stuff!"

Oliver remembered his mom was still out back. Naturally, she couldn't hear him. And Hattie and Suki had gone to watch the Lakeside varsity soccer game, which meant he couldn't get either one of them in trouble until they got back. Suki was probably in on it too, but Hattie was always the ringleader. He took pride in keeping his room tidy and his sisters always left their "messy" mark wherever they went. They didn't even think to throw away their "evidence." But Oliver was one step ahead as he'd written everything with his special ink on his notepad. His nosy sisters wouldn't have had a clue as to what he'd written. And even if they did figure it out, they'd probably think he was making it up anyway.

He took a quick glance left and right before closing his blinds completely. He couldn't believe Tattoo was Mr. Parsons. Even more frightening was that he could be watching him at this very moment with Pop's binoculars. How many times, Oliver wondered, had Mr. Parsons watched Oliver watching *him*? What had initially seemed so exciting was now truly scary. He knew that he had bitten off more than he could chew. And as more and more of his neighbors' things were taken, Oliver was really feeling more and more guilty. Of course, he'd found the key and the shed, but now the police thought Oliver was a thief. He felt he was losing control.

It was too much for him to process. His mind was racing. What should he do? Mr. Parsons had taken all his neighbors' priceless heirlooms and even though he had the proof, would it be enough?

He thought about all the hours he'd spent in the forest watching him, all the long days he'd spent in his bunker trying to make sense of it all, his truth-seeking and secret-keeping . . . and for what? His parents had always said to tell the truth, and here he was lying . . . or at least that's how it felt. His mom would understand. She'd believe him. She'd fix this . . . she always made it better.

"Oliver, the fountain is here. Can you please come outside to help?" his mom shouted up the stairs.

Oliver headed back down and out back to meet his mom and the delivery man.

"Scout, if you would put the fountain in the back of the garden, please. It's too heavy for me."

He lifted the fountain, moving it from one spot to the next because his mom kept changing her mind.

"Yes, there is perfect," said his mom.

"No, actually a little more to the right.

"There. Wait. Maybe I like it where you had it to start. Sorry, I'm having a difficult time deciding things today."

Finally, after deciding on the spot, he put it down.

"Thank you so much Scout. It's going to be so beautiful," said his Mom. "I'm off to grab us some fresh lemonade. I'll be back in a jiffy."

When his mom walked away, Oliver started busying himself with taking out all of the parts and laying them on the lawn when he heard a loud truck engine. Had the *lovely* gentleman arrived? Oliver wished he could get out of this fountain building so he could bike over to Carter's. He and Pierce were staying the night there tonight, and he decided he'd have to tell them both everything before it got any crazier. He hoped the *lovely* gentleman would insist it was a "one-person" job. He was still looking down and didn't realize the man was standing behind him until he heard him speak.

"Good evening, Mr. Morton. I feel so lucky to get to see you twice today."

Oliver didn't need to turn around to know who it was, and he looked around for his mother for support but didn't see her. What was Mr. Parsons doing here? How could this be happening? He wanted to run, but his legs were frozen.

"It seems, Mr. Morton, that you and I share a secret. Well, I want you to know that I don't plan on sharing the secret, and I surely hope you don't either. I noticed your mom has a lovely collection of Russian dolls. I bet they are pretty expensive, wouldn't you say?" Mr. Parsons stared straight at Oliver, forcing him to make eye contact.

Oliver couldn't move or speak, and just nodded. Just then, his mom came skipping over with a tray of lemonade and cookies.

"Thank you so much. I am so sorry I didn't realize you were already here. I'm Gretchen Morton and this is my son, Oliver. I'm sorry, I can't recall your name."

Oliver spoke before *he* had a chance to introduce himself.

"Mr. Parsons. His name is Mr. Parsons. He works at my school."

"Oh, how impressive. Didn't you say you were a gardener, or a landscaper, was it? So, you're a gardener *and* you also work for the school? How lovely to have a friendly face to work with, right, Oliver?"

Oliver couldn't believe this was happening. He had to get out of there.

"Uh, Mom, I need to use the bathroom," Oliver said under his breath.

"Okay, sweetie. We'll get started."

Oliver tried not to look like he was about to collapse. He wanted to run as fast as his feet would take him, but he knew he should "play it cool." He felt sweat dripping down his forehead as he leisurely headed in the back door of his house. Behind him, he could hear his mom laughing and probably apologizing for her son's *rude behavior.* But no way was Oliver going back out there, and now after their "fun fountain day," his mom wouldn't believe him either. Oliver ran upstairs, grabbed his backpack and his "PRIVATE" box, and headed to Carter's. He wanted them to know the whole story. After all of this, Oliver hoped it would make him feel better to share that he had witnessed Mr. Parsons, their friendly school janitor and local gardener, actually stealing from several of his neighbors. And that after one of his "stakeouts," Oliver had discovered a hidden key. And then upon finding the shed in Hollier's Grove, had opened the lock. And that inside the metal framed shed, Oliver found thousands and thousands of stolen goods.

Chapter Eight
THE STORY

After the visit to the principal's office, the impromptu meeting with Mr. Parsons in his back garden, and his mom's newfound "friendship" with the enemy, he was grateful to finally be sitting on Carter's bedroom floor with his two closest friends. Pierce and Carter sat quietly listening with bated breath to every word. He told them about his bunker where he'd hidden to watch *him*, and the countless hours he spent documenting all of *his* comings and goings. He told them about the shed, about the blue truck, about his tattoo. He told them everything. He didn't spare one detail. And after sharing everything, he could physically feel his body start to finally relax.

"So, the binoculars are your grandfather's, not Mr. Parsons's?" asked Carter.

"Right," said Oliver. "Those were my grandfather's, but he has the same initials as Mr. Parsons's dad. My grandfather left those to me. I have to get them back. But it seems he was always one step ahead of me. He must have seen me watching him, and now he's doing his best to try to scare me into not telling," Oliver explained.

"What are you going to do now? How will you get them back?" Pierce asked.

"That's the thing. I was hoping *we'd* get them back. I spoke to Kayden, and he's coming into town. He suggested we get a tribe together. And my cousin Patrick is coming too. I'm working on a plan, but it involves more snooping, and it might be a little dangerous. I don't know what Mr. Parsons is capable of. I'm honestly scared to be alone right now. I want to beat him at his own game, but I can't do it without you guys. What do you think? Are you two in?"

Oliver felt he had to be completely honest with the danger that could be involved, but even after hearing everything, Carter didn't even skip a beat.

"Of course, I am. You can't make this stuff up. I've been dying to do something more exciting," said Carter.

"Absolutely. I'm in. It's just so weird. I've lived here my whole life. How did we not see all of this coming?" added Pierce.

"I don't know. It's one of the things we need to find out, but I think Suit is getting nervous. That might be helpful for us," said Oliver.

"What could have happened to make Mr. Parsons want to do this to his own town? My family has trusted him for years, doing work here and there. I'm still in shock," Carter added.

"But you DO believe me?" Oliver was still a little worried that even his friends held loyalties to Mr. Parsons.

"Bro, we completely believe you. It's just crazy, that's all. He's always been a part of Lakeside so no one would suspect him," commented Pierce.

Oliver nodded in agreement.

"Yeah. He's pretty well known all over the community. I remember only a few years back when you couldn't go on a street without seeing him mowing some neighbor's yard," Carter said.

"Yeah, he was everyone's Grass Keeper; always smiling and waving. I'm sure everyone, especially our parents, will be shocked," Pierce added.

"He's the perfect unsuspecting guy to do this under everyone's noses. That's exactly why we need to have as much evidence as possible. And it will be even harder now that Principal Sanders thinks I'm the bad guy. He has no idea! And my mom knows him too now and has decided he's such a 'nice guy.' It's unreal," Oliver continued.

"So, what's next?" asked Carter.

"Next, we become detectives," Oliver said, with an almost excited tone. "Mr. Parsons told Suit that they will do one more burglary. What would be ideal is if we could actually *catch them in the act* and get a photo of both of them. My grandfather's camera has a telephoto lens that will work perfectly. And while we're talking tactics, I think Patrick should be the 'brains' of the operation. And I'm going to ask Robert and Harry too. With Kayden, that makes us a group of seven. I think if we all put our heads together, we'll actually have a chance. I thought we could meet at the bunker before school and iron out all of the details. We have a lot to do, and we need to act fast now that Tattoo knows that *I know* he's Tattoo. This isn't going to be easy, but I think the only way we will be able to stop this is with our fearless tribe."

Chapter Nine
THE BUNKER

As they all walked in and around the bunker, Oliver told the tribe everything about the robberies, Mr. Parsons—a.k.a. Tattoo—and Suit.

"Wow! So, when we've been looking for you, you've been hiding out in here in your bunker? Dude, you've been holding out. This place is awesome!" marveled Robert.

"I must have walked past it hundreds of times, can't believe I never saw it. It's the perfect hiding spot, man. I'm impressed," Harry added.

Oliver tipped his imaginary hat to accept the compliment. But of course, that's exactly why Oliver had chosen this very spot. Far, far away from any curious eyes and deep in the forest, he'd found a place no one would find . . . unless he led them there himself. The lush grass looked like a blanket, covering the forest floor. Lakeside was known for the cascading bundles of Spanish moss, and they hung from the trees that surrounded his man-made bunker. The smothered trees provided a cover for the bunker and a safe place, secretly nestled in plain sight. The blades of cattails almost pointed directly to the stones leading to the bunker door. It was as if every branch had been strategically placed to remind Oliver how to get back.

"All right, so we know who Tattoo is, but we still need to find out who the other 'thief' is," Pierce added. "Who's Suit?"

Oliver pulled out all of his "evidence" to show Patrick, Robert, and Harry what he'd already shown the others.

"So, as you can see, the houses they've hit don't seem to be in any particular order. They are *collecting* items, but there doesn't seem to be a pattern, which means there's no way of knowing where they'll hit next," said Oliver.

Carter had brought a white board and within minutes, Patrick was already working out a cataloguing system.

"We can start with what we *do* know. Here are the houses they've hit so far and a list of all of the items we've found," said Patrick.

"Yeah, and the families that we have found stolen goods for are the Smiths, the Zunigas, the Hunts, the Gunns, the Donalds, and Mr. Jackson," said Kayden.

"We should follow up with each family to see what they have reported as 'missing' to see if it matches up with what we have," added Pierce.

"And since Oliver took pictures of everything he found in the shed, I was able to organize them under each house name. The blank places indicate items we may have missed, as well as houses they may have hit that we don't even know about yet," added Patrick.

He knew Patrick would keep them on task.

"Why don't we split up so we can find answers faster?"

Robert suggested. "Kayden and I can go to the Zunigas and even the Hunts."

"And Harry and I can take the Smiths and the Donalds. They live down the street from me," added Pierce.

"Mr. Jackson lives near me. I can check in with him," said Carter.

"And I'll take the Gunns," said Oliver.

Patrick wrote all of the new information on their white board as they started planning their tactics.

"You know, being in here, planning all of this, sneaking around . . . Don't you all feel like we're kinda like *spies*?" Robert pointed out.

"Yeah. Totally. We should all have code names," Pierce added.

"We should come up with cool names like those Gladiators. What were their names again? Think there was an Ice, Rock, or was it Tank?" Harry added.

"Ooh I know who I want to be. I'll be 'Sweat,'" said Carter.

"Yeah, you're *sweaty* all right," said Robert. "And I could be 'Thunder,' and Harry, you could be 'Lightning.' Who do you want to be, Ollie?"

"You should totally be Noob, Pierce," said Kayden, and they all started laughing. "I'll be Mr. Red."

"Mr. Red doesn't even make any sense. This isn't *Among Us*," Patrick added.

"Mr. Red, as in *Red Sox*," said Kayden.

"'Noob?'" said Pierce. "Really? What's wrong with you guys? Oh yeah . . . everything."

"Ah come on, Pierce. Noob is perfect," said Carter.

"I'll be 'Scout,'" said Oliver, and as he said it aloud, he realized "Scout" did suit him, even if he was in middle school.

"Okay so now that we all have our names, what's the plan? Should we tell an adult like Mr. Jackson?" asked Harry.

"Yeah, Scout, what's the plan?" Robert added.

"We definitely need to tell an adult, and Mr. Jackson is a good person to tell, especially since we've organized this tribe 'officially' for him, but I think I know an even better person to tell," said Oliver.

"Okay, don't leave us waiting in anticipation for too long," Pierce added.

"Mrs. Fedewa. We should tell Mrs. Fedewa. She's perfect. She'll know what to do. I know we can trust her," replied Oliver.

"And Harry, you should be in charge of getting a real name for Suit. You know everyone in this town. I'll give you everything I have on him. Maybe Patrick, you could help Harry?" Oliver continued.

"Ah, everyone loves Mrs. Fedewa. She is perfect. Have you told my dad yet?" asked Robert.

"You mean the *guy who came before* 'Thunder and

Lightning?'" added Pierce, laughingly. "I seriously crack myself up."

"Nope. Not yet. We're the only ones who know. Oh, and the thieves, of course," Oliver answered.

"I'm cool with that plan and personally, I think Suit sounds like he might end up being the one in charge," Patrick replied.

"That's what I'm thinking too," Oliver echoed.

"And if we can get Mrs. Fedewa to help us, maybe Lakeside will actually listen. They won't believe it's Mr. Parsons," said Robert.

"I can only imagine who Suit is," said Harry. "I think we're in for a wild ride."

As they all gathered the boxes of evidence, Oliver looked around the bunker. These were his friends. He was beginning to realize how much he needed them. Now all they had to do was figure out a way to tell Lakeside their secret. Next stop was to see Mrs. Fedewa.

Chapter Ten
THE ALLY

The bright green color of the grass in Lakeside never seemed to fade. Abby Fedewa believed more than anyone that the sentiment, "the grass is always greener on the other side," did not apply to Lakeside. She knew the roots had flourished because of the amazing people who had always looked out for one another. And she had seen their kindness and what it meant to be part of a community firsthand when her grandparents died. They had been the very first two residents of Lakeside. Her grandfather, Mel Hollier, founded the first church in their home, and they had been the first to invest in Lakeside

Bank. Mel and Anna Hollier were permanent fixtures in the social scene that was Lakeside in the 1950s, and when they passed, Abby received an outpouring of support from everyone. She became a teacher like her mother and grandmother before her, and ended up marrying a prominent businessman from Michigan. Mrs. Fedewa was Oliver's favorite teacher and the one person who understood him. She appreciated Oliver for his kindness and honesty, and likewise, Oliver trusted Mrs. Fedewa. And perhaps because she'd not had any children of her own, Abby Fedewa was beginning to think of Oliver as the son she never had.

Oliver saw Mrs. Fedewa walk into her classroom and he motioned for everyone to follow him into her room.

"Mrs. Fedewa, we have something urgent that we need to tell you. And we *really* need your advice on what to do next," Oliver spoke in a whisper.

"Well, I see. It sounds serious. Come in, come in. Hopefully I can help," replied Mrs. Fedewa anxiously.

The boys filed into her classroom and Mrs. Fedewa shut the door behind them. And as Kayden and Oliver started to tell her what was happening, everyone tried to speak at the same time.

"One at a time. My dears, I only have two ears!" Mrs. Fedewa spoke in her famous "rhyming fashion."

English had never been a class Oliver liked back home, but

Dayly
silverbug
10

because of Mrs. Fedewa, Shakespeare was quickly becoming one of his favorite playwrights. He and the tribe proceeded to tell Mrs. Fedewa everything, trying not to leave anything out. And when they finished, she spoke very calmly.

"Before I say another word, I want to emphasize how brave I think all of you have been, especially you, Oliver. I could not have done half of the things you've managed to do. Now here's what I'm thinking . . .

"The next Town Hall is coming up and it would be the perfect place to get as many people gathered as possible. That's what you'll need . . . a room full of captive listeners . . . a packed house to fully appreciate *The Grass Keeper Chronicles.*"

"*The Grass Keeper Chronicles.*" He liked it. In fact, he thought it was perfect. So did apparently everyone else by their approving nods.

"And even better is that I'm in charge of putting the agendas together. The only issue I can see is that the Town Hall is in three days. Do you think that's enough time to put everything together?"

The group exchanged glances as Robert spoke.

"Three days isn't much time, and we still have so much to do," Robert answered.

"But we can do it. With this tribe, we can do anything," added Patrick.

They nodded in agreement.

"But what if Mr. Parsons is there?" asked Pierce.

"Yeah, and Suit," added Carter.

"There's a very good chance that both of them will be there, but it sounds as though you have so much evidence that it won't matter whether they are there or not, with the exception that it might be scarier if they are," said Mrs. Fedewa. "My plan will be to introduce y'all after the police chief. Oh, and it goes without saying but maybe bears mentioning . . . you'll need to bring your 'A' game. I'm sure there will be a lot of questions and lots of people in shock. No one will be expecting any of this."

"And there's no way these weasels can wiggle out of this one," said Kayden.

"I'm a little worried, though. Do you think Suit works for the school too?" said Robert nervously.

"If so, it's hard to know who we can trust," Carter added.

"Well, you have me and Madds . . . I mean Mr. Jackson. I haven't mentioned anything to him but will when you're ready. He might have more insight into the *comings and goings* of the male teachers here at Lakeside," Mrs. Fedewa added.

"I personally don't think Suit's the accomplice. I think he's the mastermind. And if that's true, it could go up much higher on the food chain," replied Patrick.

Everyone again nodded in agreement.

"We're going one last time to see if we can find anything that can help us figure out who this 'Suit' guy is and to gather as much evidence as we can, but we should definitely include Mr. Jackson. After all, we're in his engineering group now," added Harry.

"True. We really need to figure out who Suit is before the Town Hall, and we're running out of time," Pierce added.

"I will keep my ears and eyes open with teachers at the school. Besides Mr. Jackson, we have four other male teachers. I suppose any one of them could be involved, although I really, really hope that's not the case. These are colleagues Mr. Jackson and I've worked with for years," said Mrs. Fedewa.

"Okay we'll work on finding more evidence and the connection between Tattoo and Suit. Can we meet back here on Thursday morning?" Oliver asked.

He could tell Mrs. Fedewa was concerned with the possibility of working with *the enemy.*

"Yes. Yes, of course. Sounds great. I just couldn't be prouder of each and every one of you. I'm a big fan of this tribe. Each of you is something very special. I can't wait to see you all in action. See you all on Thursday!" added Mrs. Fedewa.

As they walked quietly down the hallways of Lakeside Middle School, they were wondering if they'd be able to pull it off. But they all agreed that they had to at least try to make right something that had gone wrong for too long.

Chapter Eleven
THE MISSION

Oliver was surprised how seriously everyone was taking their jobs, and he was becoming increasingly confident they could actually pull this off. He also thought about the fact that most of the members of this tribe had only known him for a few months and now, he couldn't imagine life without them. Oliver knew they only had one chance to get this right. At least they had Mrs. Fedewa on their side and very soon, he hoped, they'd have all of Lakeside behind them.

In an effort to not worry the neighbors any further, Harry had suggested they all use the engineering "cover story" and to not even mention the burglaries. Everyone was on pins and needles, nervous that their house might be the next target. Carter's dad ran the local hardware shop and Oliver overheard him saying that they couldn't keep locks on the shelf and that everyone was rekeying their front doors, something his company didn't even offer before. Since Mr. Parsons still had Oliver's binoculars, Carter brought Oliver a new pair, along with "night goggles," electrical tape, black clothes for them all to wear that evening, and multiple flashlights. The boys started by splitting up and going from house to house to get "theft" inventories. Pierce wrote their "scripts" to say to each family, and Patrick was in charge of adding the data, as he received it, to his already very organized dossier. Harry and Robert spent hours and hours matching the items, dates, and notes Oliver had written on his notepad with his magic ink and after adding the photos, Robert started creating their presentation. Kayden was the *tech guy* and he made sure what was created (a.k.a. the most impressive presentation any of them had ever been a part of) would be able to play at the Town Hall when the time came. Even Mr. Jackson would be proud of all of the research and proof they had collected.

"I'm honestly amazed at how much you've put into this. How did you have time for any homework?" marveled Carter.

Oliver had written every single incident with the date and the time for every robbery he witnessed. He even had specific details and drawings about Mr. Parsons's tattoo and his blue truck.

"I told you guys I had a lot. It was just so much that I wasn't sure where to start. If Mr. Parsons wasn't one step ahead of me, I would have told my parents a long time ago," Oliver explained. "It's difficult to sort through all the details."

“But what I don’t understand is, why? Why has he done this to his own neighbors and his own friends?” Patrick wondered aloud.

“That’s the million-dollar question,” replied Robert.

“I think I have an idea on how to find out who Suit is. And maybe the *why* will then be explained. But we need to find that shed!” Kayden added.

The tribe had managed to stay clear of Mr. Parsons, but the police were all over Lakeside, taking statements from all of Lakeside Middle School staff . . . including Mr. Parsons. It seemed the thieves hadn’t stopped at just one more burglary, which meant they weren’t as worried as Oliver thought they were. He knew they were all ready, but Oliver couldn’t shake the thought that Mr. Parsons might be watching them. If he knew what they were planning, he could sabotage everything. He wondered if Mr. Parsons had noticed that Oliver had been to the storage shed in Hollier's Grove before, but as evening fell, he prayed they could go undetected, find what they needed, and that they wouldn't be ambushed.

As the sun went down on what would be their last night collecting evidence, they knew they had to work fast. The Town Hall was on Thursday, so time was running out. Everything would be crucial to their success.

The November air was cool as they set off. Dressed in all black, the tribe stealthily crept to the shed. As the wind started to howl, the temperature dropped. Winter was just around the corner. They shivered from the cold air, but they knew the reward far outweighed their discomfort. The cooler weather wasn't what was bothering Oliver though. He felt the unmistakable chill to which he had become accustomed. He tried to pretend he wasn't afraid. He had convinced his friends to help him and finally here they all were . . . together. This wasn't the time to worry.

Pierce had Pop's camera, and Kayden had suggested they set up the camera to catch the thieves in action. With any movement, the camera was designed to snap a shot. When they were only a few feet from the shed, Harry motioned for everyone to stay quiet. Tattoo was in full view and Kayden's camera clicked. He didn't move so it seemed as if Tattoo hadn't heard it. It went off three more times.

Click.

Click.

Click.

They were going to be able to pull this off.

Click.

Pierce picked up Pop's camera and took a shot.

Click.

Pop's old camera made an unmistakable sound . . . an extremely *loud* sound. And then, all of a sudden, they realized Mr. Parsons had turned and was facing them. They all froze as they each tried to think of where to hide or if they should run. But before they could do anything, Suit exited the building. They could only see a dark figure. He hadn't made it as far as the light that was still illuminating Mr. Parsons's face when Pierce reached down and shot once more.

Click.

At the risk of exposing them all, they all knew it had to be done. It seemed even louder than the first shot, but shockingly, the thieves weren't looking at the boys. Maybe the tribe was wrong. Maybe Tattoo and Suit hadn't spotted them.

Suit took a step forward. He was in plain view; his profile looked almost angelic with the light hitting it.

Oliver felt blood rush to his head.

Click.

Harry gasped.

Click.

Carter motioned to stay quiet with his mouth open.

Robert dropped the flashlight, and it made a loud thud.

The tribe rushed to the nearby tree to hide and looked back. It looked as though the men were walking toward him. They all huddled closely. Oliver wished they were at the bunker right now, his safe place. But after a few minutes, they heard a car engine and then what sounded like a car, driving away. After a long pause, they all stood, speechless, looking at each other in disbelief. They had seen Suit.

"But it can't be him," said Harry. *"He* can't be Suit."

"Who is it?" asked Kayden.

No one said anything. No one knew what to say. Everyone was in shock.

"Who is it?" Kayden repeated. "Who is Suit? Is it someone you know? Someone say *something*. You guys can't do me like this."

"Carter, you tell him," said Pierce, who was busy putting away the camera parts.

"Yeah. Carter, you tell him," urged Robert. "Oh, we know him alright."

"So apparently Suit is . . ." Carter started to answer when they heard another car engine start. It sounded more like a truck; maybe Mr. Parsons was leaving. Had he seen them? It was hard to know but Oliver didn't want to stick around any longer to find out.

"We need to go . . . NOW!" said Oliver.

They all followed Oliver back to the road, walking in silence. The reality of what they'd seen was finally sinking in. They had stumbled into a spider's web that would rock the entire community. The photos Pierce had taken would be irrefutable. *Good luck talking your way out of this one*, Oliver thought to himself.

Chapter Twelve
TOWN HALL

As Lakeside residents trickled into the Town Hall, the tribe stayed behind, waiting for their introduction. Mrs. Fedewa said for them to listen out for "Open Door." Oliver's nerves were on edge and he didn't want to miss his cue. As they waited patiently, the police chief started the meeting.

"Order, please. Order. Let's come to order," spoke Police Chief Polan.

It seemed everyone was at the Town Hall, but as he scanned the room, he noticed two obvious absentees. Oliver also saw the Hunts, the Donalds, the Smiths, the Zunigas, the Gunns, and Mr. Jackson and his husband. The tribe busied themselves pulling together their presentation materials so they'd be ready as Chief Polan continued.

"I know the last Town Hall was at the start of all these terrible robberies, and I wish I could say we were closer to catching those involved, but unfortunately, I cannot with any certainty say that. We will be relentless on finding out how this has happened in our quiet community and apprehend those responsible. I know we are all very angry, and many of us are equally worried. But I want to reassure you that we now have a task force that will be handling this, and it is our number one priority. At this point, I will now hand the microphone over to the head of the history department at Lakeside High School, Mr. Franklin."

"Thank you, Lyle. So, I want you to all know that we are also making consorted efforts at the high school to find out anything we can. We have conducted locker searches, spoken to the staff, and increased our campus security. We will catch this thief—or thieves. On a side note, my own house was hit last night, so I am probably even more fueled than I was before, if that's possible. I want to now hand over the mic to the head of Lakeside Middle School's English department, Mrs. Fedewa . . . Abby?"

"Good evening everyone and thank you Mr. Franklin. Like you, I want to also promise you all that Lakeside Middle

School is doing our very best to continue to make your children feel safe at school, as well continuing to gather relevant information. Not to go without saying . . . your children's safety is our main concern. We are all in this together and we will make Lakeside safe again. We have increased security, conducted locker searches, and have recently introduced our 'Open Door' policy. 'Open Door' allows children to write messages anonymously and put them in my box at school. If they want me to contact them directly, they only need put that on the sheet. In fact, days ago we spoke with a student who has some vital information to share with us. I'd now like to welcome to the podium my wonderful student, Oliver Morton. Oliver? Are you here?"

Everyone scanned the room as the tribe headed down the long walkway with boxes in their hands. Patrick rolled a cart with a television. As they reached the front of the room, they exchanged glances. They all hoped their neighbors would believe what they were about to tell them because it really was hard to believe.

"Thank you, Mrs. Fedewa. My name is Oliver Morton, but my friends call me 'Scout.'"

Oliver and the rest of the tribe stood on the stage with their *evidence*, ready to prove they knew the thief or thieves.

"And this is Patrick, Carter, Pierce, Robert, Kayden, and Harry. Many of you have spoken to us over the past few days and we wouldn't have been able to build this case without you. And for full disclosure, while we are an engineering group through school, our tribe has also been gathering evidence that we want to share with you all. If we can please have your full attention. We think you will all be surprised to hear what we've found."

"We are here in front of you all today because we have found all of your stolen items," said Pierce.

The neighbors gasped and started talking quietly to one another as Carter pulled out the whiteboard.

"We have also discovered who is responsible for the burglaries—and we have proof," Patrick added.

Under each set of items, Harry put the family name, as well as the date and time the burglary had occurred. Oliver could tell people were in shock, and they could hear people crying and even a few claps as they continued talking about how they had spent months obtaining the evidence and how fearful they were at first to come forward.

"As you see, we have brought back an item from each of your houses to show you we aren't just kids with active imaginations," Oliver added.

"And the rest of your items are safe in a storage shed only two miles away in Hollier's Grove," said Kayden as he showed a photo of the shed.

"There are only three keys to that storage facility, and we have one. The other two keys are in the possession of . . . well this is when it gets a bit tricky," Pierce added as he looked around to see if Tattoo or Suit had snuck in when they weren't looking.

"Would you all like to know the names of the thieves that have been taking things from us and keeping us all in a state of fear for the last few months?" asked Patrick.

"Yes, we do!" Everyone chimed in unison.

With that, Carter put up one of the two slides with names and titles underneath the photo. The first one they showed was the school janitor and local gardener, Mr. Parsons. He had worked in all of the schools over the years and in almost as many people's gardens. Everyone knew Mr. Parsons.

"Although it seems Mr. Parsons conveniently isn't here tonight, I am happy to tell you that he was the one stealing all of your things. I watched him on many nights stealing and storing them. But it wasn't until last night that we discovered his accomplice," said Oliver.

Carter then showed their last and final slide, and everyone was in complete shock because the last slide was a big photo of their very own Principal Ethan Sanders. Many people stood and looked around to see if Principal Sanders was in the room, but he wasn't there.

"That's right. We believe Mr. Sanders was the mastermind of the whole ordeal. After we discovered he was the other thief, we did a little more snooping and discovered he had a file with all of your names and addresses, as well as a list of valuable contents in your homes," said Robert.

"We suspect he gained access when he did his home visits at the start of each school year," Harry added.

"And it wouldn't take much to jot down the items and in which rooms they resided, but that last part is only speculation," Patrick concluded.

When the boys had finished, the room went completely silent. They waited with anticipation as Police Chief Lyle Polan stood up and started clapping. And one by one, so did every single person in the room.

"And I have even more good news to share with you all. I've issued arrest warrants for Mr. Parsons and Principal Sanders. Oliver, for your bravery and hard work, the city of Lakeside owes you a debt of gratitude," spoke the chief. "Please, let's all give the tribe another round of applause. All of us want to thank you for everything you've done."

The cheering continued as the boys made their way to the outstretched arms of their proud parents.

"We can't believe you boys did all of this. You worked so

hard, but why didn't you tell us? Maybe we could have helped you," said Gretchen Morton.

"We were worried you wouldn't believe us," Oliver replied.

"How could we not believe you, Scout? You're just like Pop and always have been. We've always known that," Corrin Morton added.

"I don't know. I guess I thought you'd think I was 'snooping' and I wanted to make a difference. I wanted to do something that Pop would be proud of. And without these guys, I wouldn't have had the courage to continue," Oliver replied.

"Well, I know that Pop would be so incredibly proud of you—but not nearly as proud of you as we are, Scout," added his mom.

"I think I finally found *my people,* Mom," said Oliver.

"I think you have too, Scout. I definitely think you have. I love you so much," his mom said.

As the tribe received accolades from their parents and the community, they all smiled proudly. This was their first *adventure* together as the tribe, but it definitely wouldn't be their last.

About the Author

Nancy Shakespeare is thrilled to release her tenth published children's book and her first chapter book. *The Grass Keeper Chronicles* was written for her youngest son, Oliver, an inquisitive adventurer and dyslexic thinker. Known mainly for her fictional writing, Nancy finds inspiration in all things magical and is a passionate storyteller. When not writing a book, poem, or song, Nancy can be found reading at local schools, creating lotions and potions with essential oils, or dancing and singing loudly in her lounge with her family and friends. Nancy and her husband, Steve, currently live in Houston, Texas, with their three children.

About the Illustrator

Marie Legrand is a traditional illustrator born in the south of France in Aix-en-Provence. She is deeply inspired by nature, fairy tales, and her two adorable children. After graduating with a master of design, she has left her mark across a broad range of industries including fashion, luxury products, movie production, and performing arts. Since devoting herself to painting and illustration, her work has been featured in set decorations, graphic design, and children's books. She also creates commission paintings. She currently lives in Houston, Texas.